# Telling Your
# Arkansas Stories

# Also by Donald Davis

**Books**
*Listening for the Crack of Dawn*
*Barking at a Fox-Fur Coat*
*Southern Jack Tales*
*See Rock City*
*Ride the Butterflies*
*Thirteen Miles from Suncrest*
*Jack and the Animals*

**Audiocassettes** (selected)
*Southern Bells*
*Listening for the Crack of Dawn*
*Party People*
*Grandma's Boy*
*Dr. York, Miss Winnie and the Typhoid Shot*
*Christmas at Grandma's*
*That's What Mamas Do*
*Miss Daisy*

**This special edition** of the classic *Telling Your Own Stories* was created especially for use in the state of Arkansas. Most of the pages of the national category bestseller are reprinted here in their entirety, with the addition at the beginning and at the end of special text that will be of interest to Arkansans.

# Telling Your
# Arkansas Stories

*For Family and Classroom
Storytelling, Public Speaking,
and Personal Journaling*

**DONALD DAVIS**

*August House Publishers, Inc.*
LITTLE ROCK

©1993, 2002 by Donald Davis.
All rights reserved. This book, or parts thereof,
may not be reproduced in any form without permission.

Published 2002 by August House Publishers, Inc.,
P.O. Box 3223, Little Rock, AR 72203, 501-372-5450
www.augusthouse.com

Printed in the United States of America
10 9 8 7 6 5 4 3 2 1

ISBN 0-87483-680-8

This book is printed on archival-quality paper that meets the guidelines for performance and durability of the Committee on Production Guidelines for Book Longevity of the Council on Book Resources.

This special edition of
*Telling Your Arkansas Stories*
was produced in collaboration with the
Department of Arkansas Heritage.
The mission of the department is to
preserve and promote Arkansas heritage
as a source of pride and satisfaction.
The department is comprised of six
agencies: the Arkansas Arts Council, the
Arkansas Historic Preservation Program,
the Arkansas Natural Heritage Commission,
the Delta Cultural Center, the
Historic Arkansas Museum and the
Old State House Museum.

# Governor's Message

We might not have realized it at the time, but growing up in Arkansas was something special. We were so involved in the process of growing up we couldn't step back and realize how lucky we were to be Arkansans.

When we reach a certain age, we inherit the gift of perspective. Because of that perspective, I now realize how blessed I was to grow up in Arkansas. Growing up in Hope was especially great. I remember what it felt like to be with my dad enjoying the outdoors. I remember my friends and the games we played. I remember my high school graduation, playing bass in my first band and many more activities and events that led me to where I am today.

Our heritage as Arkansans is in the stories we carry with us. I encourage you to capture the memories of what growing up in Arkansas was like. Pass the stories on to your children. Write them down for others. At some point, people of every generation want to know more about their past. Your stories, preserved in voice or the written word, will ensure that those who come after us will always be able to learn about that past.

*Mike Huckabee,*
*Governor of Arkansas*

# Welcome

Growing up in Arkansas. What a unique and wonderful experience it is. No matter whether that growth spans many decades or merely one, it is interwoven with stories that give character and depth to what might otherwise be simply a chronology of events. Heritage is history portrayed through the eyes of those who were there. Preserving our family memories through our stories is an important way of preserving the richness of our past. That's why we chose *Growing Up In Arkansas: Everyone Has a Story* as the theme for Heritage Month 2002, and why we've partnered with August House on this book to help us remember and record the stories we all have.

With the help of this book, you will find just how powerful a simple story can be. What may begin as a fragment of a memory, dim and threadbare with age, will emerge from the smoke like a dream.

Whether by word of mouth or the written word, we must preserve these stories if we are to understand how we came to be who we are, and shape any kind of enduring future for ourselves and our children.

Preserving, restoring, discovering and promoting our state's past — in the present — is what the Department of Arkansas Heritage is all about. The six agencies that comprise the department each have an important challenge. Their challenge is one of assuring that future generations will be able to appreciate the art, artifacts, flora, fauna, land forms, architecture, people and events that made our state what it is...no matter whether that is today, next year or a hundred years from today.

We are proud of Arkansas, and we love to tell her stories.

*Cathie Matthews,*
*Director, Department of Arkansas Heritage*

# Preface

Whenever we put together our own stories and either tell them or write them for posterity, we are preserving the most central element of our own identity and value system. Who are we, apart from the people and the events about which we tell in our own stories?

Our stories tell us, our family members, our neighbors and our descendants more about who we are than do all of the assembled lists of our educational and professional accomplishments combined. When we go back to the house after the funeral, what do we do? We tell stories about the deceased in order to celebrate and remember!

If this is true, why is it so difficult for us to work at finding, remembering, and writing or telling these stories about ourselves and our families? Perhaps it is because familiarity breeds not contempt, but boredom! Our own lives and our own home places are so very familiar to us that we do not imagine that the things we have done could possibly be of interest or importance to other people.

This is a universal problem. No matter where people live, the mere familiarity of home tricks us into a belief that there are no interesting stories in our places or in our lives.

In traveling as a storyteller and workshop leader, I have had these experiences: schoolchildren in Orange County, Florida, who can see the top of Cinderella's Castle from their schoolyard think they live in a boring place because there is nothing to do but go to Disney World *again!* Residents of a village on the North Slope of Alaska are certain their lives (traveling to school by dogsled or on snowmobiles) are boring because they have no McDonald's in their village! All of us think that the place we live is surely boring, or else why would we have ended up there? The familiar becomes boring, no matter where we live.

If we are to find Arkansas stories, our first task is to realize that Arkansas is not a boring place!

As I have worked in almost every corner of the state I have come to be amazed by the potential richness of life and stories about living that I meet in Arkansas. Let me tell you of some of my thoughts about your state and see whether these thoughts might dust some story memories from the corners of your mind.

Arkansas's location within the United States is amazingly unique. Your state reaches from the Mississippi River, just across bridges from Tennessee (a markedly Southeastern state) all the way to Oklahoma (with cowboys, Cherokee people, and modern vestiges of the frontier). It ranges from the highlands of the north to true Delta country as you travel southeast.

There are few parts of our nation in which we can cover such a variety of physical geography in a single state. Have you moved about the state in your life and experienced some of this variety?

In addition to the multiplicity of surface area features and the range of geographic reach, Arkansas varies from forests on top of the ground to a vast array of mineral resources just a few feet below — even a diamond mine preserved in a state park.

Do you have, in your own family memories, or in your personal experience, any Mississippi River stories? Any Ozark stories? How about mineral-water stories or diamond stories? These are stories unique to Arkansas among all of our states.

Arkansas is a state of diverse national business origins and headquarters. Where else in this country could you find people at a family reunion talking about their jobs at the headquarters of WalMart, Jacuzzi, Dillards, J.B. Hunt, Tyson Foods, or many other unique Arkansas businesses? Where have you worked, in Arkansas, for your own working life? Are there stories to be told about those employment experiences?

Arkansas is also a state rich in history. Few other states have a history of French and Spanish occupation prior to United States history, and even fewer can claim to have been visited by DeSoto, Marquette and Jolliet, and LaSalle as well as other early explorers. Does your family ancestry contain roots that reach back into early historic periods? Have you searched for these stories and tried to preserve them for your descendants?

Does your family have historic memories of, or connections with, time periods such as the "Trail of Tears" or the civil rights era of school desegregation?

Then, there is the whole world of Arkansas politics! Maybe you have some stories there. There is no other state in which the residents can claim to have had the first female member of the United States Senate. It was Hattie Caraway, who in 1932 went to the Senate in a special election following her husband's death, who will hold that record for Arkansas forever! Are there still living members of your family who remember that?

If not, as we move through political history, surely stories will come as we dust our memories with names like Orval Faubus, Winthrop Rockefeller, and on down the years to Bill and Hillary Clinton and Jim Guy Tucker. Do you have family stories sparked by thinking about any of these Arkansas "characters"? What about local politics and your family's relationship to those stories?

Arkansas is full of stories!

Whether you live in Little Rock or Smackover, whether you were born in Mena or Mountain Home, whether your family came from Beebe or Crystal Springs, you have stories.

State fairs? County fairs? Tornadoes? Floods? Ice storms? As you enter the pages of this book, you may well find long-forgotten stories about all of them.

Give it a try, and see what joy you, your family, your neighbors, and, some day, your descendants will gain when they hear you say, "Let me tell you a story about Arkansas!"

*— Donald Davis*

# Dee Brown...My Arkansas Memories

Many elders in your community — and at ninety-four I suppose I count myself among them — are reluctant to talk about the past out of age-old performance anxiety: we're afraid we will bore you to death. But the past century has brought about advances and events of enormous importance, and your elders were there to witness them. It's vital for a society to pass down stories and memories from one generation to the next, and you can be a part of that chain. I hope you will use some of the ideas in this book to prompt an older relative or friend or neighbor to tell you about their past. I assure you they will respond once they know you are genuinely interested.

Here are just a few of my own memories and anecdotes I don't believe I've ever set down in writing before.

# ■ Magazines ■

When I was a boy in Stephens, Arkansas, the outside world sifted into our community slowly. The term "broadcast journalism" would not become a figure of daily speech for another fifty years. What I remember was magazines. Pulp magazines cost a dime apiece, and the slicks were more expensive. Most of them were household magazines.

My mother subscribed to two or three of these, things like *Women's Home Companion* and *Ladies' Home Journal.* Her sisters and sisters-in-law, who lived nearby, subscribed to similar magazines. Every month each magazine made a circuit among the homes, being read first in the home of the subscriber and then passed on to a sister — one of my many aunts then resident in Stephens. The Browns, the Criners, and the Tutts were all related, and it made a great reading club as the magazines made their way from house to house, with each of us reading with the cleanest fingers possible.

The pulp magazines carried stories, household tips, and patent medicine ads. The cheaper the magazine, the more medicines were advertised. They seemed to offer cures for everything. Slick magazines had fewer such ads; their advertisers wanted to sell you bigger things: wringer washing machines and other modern contrivances to use in household chores. Every once in a while you would see an automobile ad in the slicks, but never in the pulps.

The magazines brought us a little literature of the day. Household magazines serialized popular authors. I particularly remember Rex Beach, who wrote adventure tales set in the north of Canada. Each of the big publishing houses had its own literary magazine. *Harper's Magazine* was very popular, as were *Scribner's* and *Macmillan's*. It was in *Scribner's* that I first read Hemingway. The literary magazines weren't as common in Stephens as the ladies' magazines were, but we cherished them and passed them around.

## ■ Erector Set Motor ■

Beginning when I was about eight, and for several years thereafter, I would ask for an electric motor for my Erector Set. Motors could transform them into so many things — a steam shovel, a Ferris wheel, anything a boy could imagine. Every year I would campaign for an electric motor for my Erector Set. For the first several years, I was denied not by my mother but by circumstance; power lines hadn't come to Stephens yet. Then when I was about thirteen, Harvey Couch's crew ran the first electric line to Stephens from the dam at Lake Catherine. I was sure I would finally get an electric motor for my Erector Set. When Christmas came, there was no motor. I was sorely disappointed, but my mother was consoled by an aunt who said she had read somewhere about a boy being electrocuted by an electric motor attached to a toy set.

## ■ Our Unforgettable Pet ■

When he came to live in our yard, he was a fluffy little white ram. He was gentle, even cuddly. He ran around the yard with cats, dogs, chickens, my cousins and myself. But the day came when his genetics took hold. Actually, I will admit that his genetics were probably drawn into play by the taunts and perhaps some blows from us boys. Somehow we must have sensed that we could, so to speak, get his goat. We just didn't realize how quickly we would get rammed!

The yard at that time was strewn with large pipes of fired clay. The pipes were nearly as tall as a boy — perfect for running through while bent over and even more perfect for playing "king of the mountain." We would tease that ram and then run through — or better, jump on top of — those pipes, for it is pipes that they were, waiting there along the street to become culverts or some such.

Occasionally, the ram would run the footrace and a little boy — myself or a cousin — would be butted in the bottom. The injuries were never serious — at least not until the day the ram struck me in the sit-upon place as I was tottering to the top of my "mountain." His blow threw me over the other side of the large pipe and dumped me onto several larger-than-usual rocks. Throwing an arm forward to protect my head, I landed with all of my weight — and velocity — on that arm, and those rocks.

*Dee Brown's "My Arkansas Memories" are continued on page 129*

To my brother, Joe –
who was there when the stories all started.

# SECTION I

## Introduction To Family Storytelling

Family stories–almost every family has them. Told at gatherings of the relatives or the extended family, they are those stories about "the time when" that help a family define their identity and stay in touch with who they are.

Many of us remember family stories as being told by older family members who, in their later life, recounted their own formative adventures time after time until they became either outlandish or boring. On the other hand, most of us wish that we had somehow preserved more of those stories that we know we heard but cannot quite recall now.

We tend to forget that *we* might have our own stories to tell as well. We wish that we had preserved the stories of Grandma but miss the fact that, for our own children and grandchildren (and even for our own generation), *we* are the ones who must be the storytellers if there is to be a richness of family stories in years to come.

Our response to this assertion is often, "But, I have no stories to tell! Nothing ever happened to me! I didn't live way back then when the world was interesting. Besides, I'm just not much of a talker anyway."

If you harbor such misgivings, this workbook is for you. *Telling Your Own Stories* was not designed for those who already have a head full of stories that are presently being told. No, it is for those who long for family storytelling but live with the misconception that they have no stories to tell. This workbook operates under the premise that all stories are about memorable **people, places, or happenings**. If, in your life and that of your family, there have been such people, places, and happenings, then there are stories to be found.

The processes set forth in *Telling Your Own Stories* are a set of baited fishhooks for you to use in a pond of stories that has probably been virtually untouched, and is uniquely yours. Use it alone if you must. Better still, use it at those times when as much of your extended family as possible gets together. It may be just the thing to replace television on those long afternoons after the holiday meal has been eaten!

# SECTION II

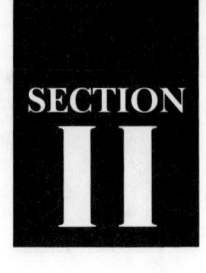

## Let's Go Fishing For Plots!

The preceding introduction pointed out that many family stories revolve around important events. In literary terminology, this means that these are stories which are plot-centered. In this section of the workbook, we will work with a set of plot prompts which are designed to help us fish for those stories which are event-centered.

The central hinge of any story plot is a **crisis**. We must be careful, however, that we do not define the term "crisis" too narrowly.

It is tempting to think of crisis in terms of heart attacks, house fires, job losses, death, and any number of other uninvited events which disrupt the course of one's hoped-for life history. But a crisis is not just an involuntary event which overtakes us against our will.

A crisis is any happening which takes a part of our lives with which we are comfortable and turns it upside down so that we have to adjust to a world that is shaped differently than before. This means that many of the most significant crises in our family lives are crises we volunteer for.

Under this definition, winning the lottery is a crisis. It requires that our whole relationship to the world be changed. Getting married is a crisis, as is having a baby, retiring, buying a new house, and all the other "choices" we gladly make. Remember this as we look at the upcoming plot prompts which we will use to try to recall simple events that may have more than simple significance.

If possible, use the prompts in a group or family setting so that there is an audience to which to tell the story that the prompt pulls from your memory. Later on it may be possible to work with prompts by yourself for your own journaling or writing.

Note that a prompt is not an assignment. The metaphor of a baited fishhook has already been used and it is again appropriate here. You may be fishing for one thing, when you unexpectedly and happily catch something else! The point is not to define a story, simply to catch one.

Take the prompts either in turn, by having each family member read one and then having that same person respond to it, or read the prompt and then see who comes up with a story first. Always check to see how many family members come up with a memory evoked by each prompt. Use the blank space on the page not to write the stories but to make brief memory notes such as "Aunt Mary told about the time when

## SECTION II

she...." so that, if not completely told or remembered now, there will be a clue to help you come back to the story and work on it more fully later.

Don't hurry! It often takes sitting with a prompt for a few minutes of thought for it to be productive. Try the prompts one at a time and see how many crisis memories your family happens to come up with before moving too quickly on to the next prompt.

Try this:

*When we try to remember, we often search from the present backwards chronologically. The problem with this is that we don't yet know how recent events are going to come out. This means that they are too raw for us to be able to either laugh or cry about them. Instead, with these prompts, try for earliest memories and then come forward. Our whole life is our library where personal memories are the books we are looking for.*

## PROMPT 1

**Can you remember a pet you once had which you don't have anymore?**

**MORE IDEAS**

How many family members remembered the same pet? Different pets? Were there stories about pets which some family members never even knew existed?

*Be sure that when a person begins to tell his or her story, others let him or her tell it! If you have memories about the same event, then your memories make a different story. Listen to the one whose story begins first, then don't correct but simply tell your story and laugh about the difference!*

## PROMPT 2

**Can you remember a time when you tried to cook something and it didn't turn out?**

**MORE IDEAS**

You may notice that it is helpful to the listener for the storyteller to be quite specific about time and place when telling his or her story. If a story begins with something like, "When I was twelve years old we were visiting at grandmother's house," it is very easy for the listener to quickly visualize time and place and to follow more clearly the event sequence which is being described.

# SECTION II

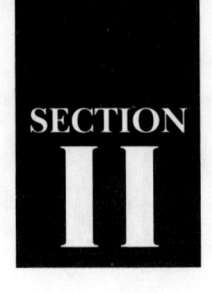

## More About Time and Place

For most of us who have grown up being taught that if we can summarize the plot we must have read the story, it seems that plot is so identical with story itself that the story almost equals the plot. But, trying to listen to an oral story which is simply made of plot is quite like trying to carry water in your hands. When there is no container, the plot, like the water, simply runs out of our listening "hands."

Whenever we, as story listeners, get ready to hear a story we have not heard before, our subconscious mind is getting ready to try to make sense out of the story for us. Before the storyteller begins to talk it seems that our mind is blank. But, while it is devoid of content, there are certain questions being asked by our subconscious listening faculties to help us follow and make sense of what we are hearing.

Contrary to our first thoughts, the initial question is not "I wonder what is going to happen in the story I am about to hear?" No, happening is plot, and before we can carry plot, our mind needs to build a container for it.

The first question the unconscious mind asks is "I wonder where the story I am about to hear is going to happen?" Once I can make a picture of "where" in my listening mind, I have a way to "see" the story and make sense of it. Part of "where" is "when." The time setting of the story is part of what we picture in our heads before anything begins to happen in the story in terms of what we would call the plot.

After we have a clear picture in our heads of the place and time in which the story is to occur, our unconscious mind can ask "I wonder who the characters in this story are going to be?"

Once we can "see" place, time, and character (including identification of the main character), we have a mental container in which to visually carry the plot of the story. We can actually see the story unfold in our heads once we have built the background places and the central people in the story. Now, if we know that as listeners we need this person- and place-container to help us carry the plot of the story, it is much easier as tellers to give our listeners such needed help when we are telling our stories.

Give attention to carefully laying out the place, the time, and the people in your stories before anything starts to happen, and begin to notice not only how much more attentively your listeners are at the moment, but also how much easier it is for you to keep track of where you are in the story and how much more clearly those who heard you tell it can remember it after hearing.

# PROMPT 3

**Can you remember a time when you got into trouble for something you had already been told not to do?**

**MORE IDEAS**

This prompt is a good one to help us realize that crises are not just those things that creep up and grab us from behind, but that many of the crisis events in our lives are the results of our own choices. What are some of the crisis events that members of your family like to volunteer for over and over again?

## SECTION II

## More about the Crisis Center of All Stories

**Crisis** is the plot center of all stories. Without a crisis to be experienced and endured by the main character, we may have a portrait but we do not really have a story.

There is, however, often an inadequate understanding of what the word crisis really means. When we hear the word, we often jump to a quick everyday definition in which we think of crisis as an unavoidable interference. While unvolunteered-for events such as illness, accidents, war, house fires, job losses, family abandonments, and others are certainly crisis events, these neither exhaust nor define the full range of crisis events which have an impact on our lives and center our life stories. A broader definition of crisis is needed.

In terms of story, a crisis is simply **any event or happening that takes a part of the world we have grown comfortable living with and turns it upside down**. Such a crisis event requires that we make adjustments to a new world as a part of living with such critical change.

Given this definition, positive changes and chosen changes are just as much crisis events as are those disturbances which are either negative or outside our field of choices. With this understanding, we come to see that winning the lottery is a crisis event! It requires that we adjust our lives very radically to live in a world quite different from the old world we lived in before our good luck.

So, getting married is a crisis event, graduating from college is a crisis event, buying a new house is a crisis event, as are having a baby, getting a job promotion, going on a dream vacation, beginning a long-awaited retirement, and a host of other changes which we choose–as well as those which creep up on us.

Many of the most significant formative stories in our family story cycle come from our recognition of the crisis nature of these positive and chosen life changes.

Notice such positive crisis events as you search for your family's stories. Notice also how repeated crisis cycles often appear in life stories. Families and individuals often choose favorite crises and go through them over and over again. Once a crisis is successfully coped with, it is much easier to face it again than to have to learn to deal with a brand new change. So we see repeated patterns, ranging from addictive behavior to constant moving to repeated job changes to perpetual schooling, as chosen crisis patterns which are more comfortable than stepping into a world of uncertain changes.

Thinking thoroughly through the widest possible range of crisis events can greatly expand the possibilities for story discovery as we review our personal and family memories.

**PROMPT 4**

Can you remember a time when you broke something that belonged to someone else?

**MORE IDEAS**

Any story is more believable if the listener can see trouble coming before the crisis actually arrives. Work at trying to include background and some of the reasons which brought on the crisis event rather than jumping into it too quickly.

## PROMPT 5

## Can you remember a trip that you would not want to have to take again?

**MORE IDEAS**

Begin to notice the ways that different people use *descriptive skills*. Observe that we can create a scene, describe a person, re-create an event, not just through telling about what would be seen, but also by making use of descriptive *smells, sounds, tastes, and tactile sensations*.

Experiment with entering a scene through sound or describing a person through smell.

# SECTION II

## More about Learning to Use Our Descriptive Skills

We have seen again and again the importance of concrete description in our storytelling. The more clearly the listener can see where we are, when we are, and who we are within the story, the more clearly those events which make up the plot can be followed and identified with.

One word which we often use to describe the phenomenon which occurs when there is good description is the word *visualize*. If we, when we are listeners, can visualize the story, then the teller's descriptive skills are being used effectively.

The term is, however, very misleading when we use it alone to cover what we are trying to achieve in our storytelling. If we say that we, as good storytellers, want to be "visualization enablers," that is a good, but very limited, term.

The problem with the word *visualize* is that it is like having five crayons to color with and then using only one of them over and over again. If our descriptive goal is merely to enable visualization, then we are making use of only one of our senses when we have five to work with.

Being people with five senses rather than just one, we can not only **see** stories as they are told, we can also mentally **smell, sound, taste**, and **touch**, if the teller makes use of these "colors" in creating the fabric of the story.

Let's think about a few examples of this. **Smell**, for instance, is a very evocative sense in our memories.

Everything has a smell and the mention of that sense in connection with a memory almost always makes connections. Remember being hugged by your mother? Do you remember her smell? Remember emptying the pencil sharpener at school? Does the inside of a pencil sharpener have a smell? Do your hands have a smell after you have been counting money? How many smells does your dog have? Dog breath? Wet dog in the house out of the rain?

Now, in a story, try to take the listeners into a scene through smell. Could you take us into your grandmother's kitchen on Thanksgiving Day through the smells that we would meet as we entered there? Try, in any scene in a story, to ask yourself whether there are smells associated with that scene which evoke a response from the listener that is greater than visualization. Do the same when describing people.

Smell is a powerful color to use in description.

Now what about **sound**?

We are often not very aware of the sounds which help to form the background of all of the important places where we live and work. But invoking reminders of these sounds in the storytelling process can greatly enhance the listeners' ability to mentally create an experience of the story being heard.

Check out your world now just to see how many sounds are there which you are not presently noticing. Close your eyes, right where you are, and start making mental note of all of the sounds you can hear around you. Is there music or television, even though you are in a different room or place from those who are playing or watching? Are there other mechanical sounds such as heat, fans, or air conditioning? Is there car, truck, or airplane noise?

What about the sounds of nature? Can you hear birds, dogs, or just the wind in the trees? Are there water sounds? If the weather were different, or if it were a different time of year, would the sounds you hear in this same place be different? Try going outside the place where you are just now and spend a bit of time listening to the outdoor sounds in which the place is bathed.

We often rely on our eyes so much that we listen to the sounds around us only when they warn us of danger. These unnoticed sounds are, however, still being recorded into our memories–and the memories of past events are full of sounds.

If you are telling a story set in the house where you grew up, could you have us sit on the front porch and listen to the sounds of the evening? Could you take us into the room where you slept through the sounds you heard when you woke up in the mornings? Can you use sound to help us "see" the car you learned to drive on, and to recreate that learning experience?

Sound can be a powerful and bright color to use when

painting the pictures which hold our stories.

The third often-unused descriptive sense is that of **taste**. Now that we have worked with smell and sound, taste is not as hard to get hold of. Just imagine recreating your grandmother's kitchen through the remembered tastes of Thanksgiving dinner.

Taste is a more appropriate sense to use in describing your favorite Girl Scout cookie, a special pizza, or a special chocolate dessert than is any other sense!

Perhaps the most difficult sense to make use of in our descriptive storytelling is the sense of **touch**. In trying to invoke touch, it is helpful to remember that we touch with our whole body surface and not just with our fingers.

Heat and cold are experiences of touch, as is the feel of the wind in our face or a grain of sand in our eye. Pain is usually experienced through touch, as are many pleasures.

More subtle uses of touch include the way it felt when your mother picked you up from sleep or your first hint that the hot water was running out in the shower just as your hair was filled with shampoo.

Senses other than sight can be great fun to use in storytelling. Experiment with using a sense other than the one you would normally use in creating a particular vision, and see how this sensory crossover enhances what the listeners experience.

## PROMPT 6

# Can you remember a party or a date you didn't want to go on to begin with?

**MORE IDEAS**

This is a good prompt for practicing the art of *caricature*. Caricature is the artistic ability to capture a whole personality using a minimum number of brush strokes, or, in storytelling, to depict a whole person with the smallest possible number of words. Caricature may be humorous but is always respectful, as opposed to stereotyping which is often negative and lacks respect. Try to describe a person you once dated *using only one sentence* so that others will get the picture of a full person when that sentence is finished.

# PROMPT 7

## Can you remember a night your parents never found out about?

**MORE IDEAS**

One thing that is hard to do in family storytelling is to remember to fully describe the people and places *even if those who are hearing the story already know those people and places.* The way in which you see the person or the place is a part of your unique story. Try telling the story as if you were telling it to someone from a faraway state who could not possibly have seen the places or people involved. Notice how interesting the perspective of the teller is as a part of even a familiar story.

## PROMPT 8

Can you remember a time when you got sick at a very inconvenient moment?

**MORE IDEAS**

When we look at a photograph we see not only the scene captured by the photographer but we also see *where the photographer stood to take the picture*. Look for this same point-of-view phenomenon in the stories you are hearing. Notice how when a person tells a story from childhood, the teller may appear to become a child again. Also notice how *emotions and prejudices* are parts of our point of view.

# SECTION II

# A Story-Form Format

You may be beginning to notice that most of the stories you are telling and hearing are similar in pattern or form even if they are quite different in content. Let's look at one version of a simple story-form format so that you can examine whether you are already seeing most of the following important elements emerging naturally in the stories you are finding in your family. Sometimes when a story doesn't quite work it may be because one or more of the components in the scheme which follows is missing. This format is not a sacred formula, it is just a check-screen to help us find holes in our stories which may be more easily filled in once we know where they are.

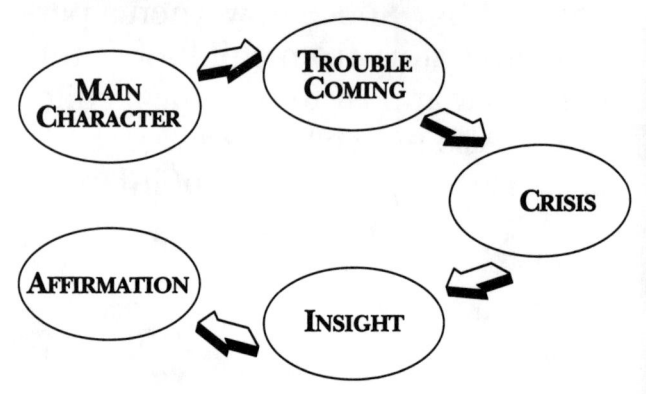

MAIN CHARACTER → TROUBLE COMING → CRISIS → INSIGHT → AFFIRMATION

In every story we meet a main character who lives in a clearly described time and place. There may be other characters, but the main character stands out from all of them and is usually a character who has something to learn. The narrator may also be the main character.

Once we meet the main character we very soon begin to get the sense that trouble is coming. We begin to see some of the main character's flaws of judgment and/or information and we know that a crisis is on the way, though we do not yet know what it is.

Now the crisis comes. We watch the main character enter and go through all of the throes of the critical event.

In the process of living through the crisis, the main character either gets help or learns something new which enables survival of the crisis. This help or learning is something which could never have been acquired apart from struggling through this particular critical event.

Once this new learning or insight has been acquired by the main character, life is, in some way, never the same. The end of the story often comes when a recurrence of the same crisis is successfully met or when there is a "forever after that" affirmation of some sort.

# SECTION II

## Let's Check On Where We Are...

Now, think back to some of the stories that you have told and heard and observe whether some or all of these elements are present in them. Notice whether some of the stories which have all of these elements, though not necessarily in chronological order, seem to be fuller and more finished than those which are missing one critical part or another.

Are there some stories you now want to tell over again? Or, does this format help you at the stage which comes when you want to record or write your stories for possible preservation?

Now that you have worked through the initial series of plot- prompts, here is a supplemental list of such starting places for further use. You should also try to make up your own crisis prompts now that you have a sense of what "catches a good memory."

## PROMPT 9

Can you remember a birthday or a holiday you would like (or not like) to live over again?

## PROMPT 10

Can you remember a time when you got lost? Or separated from your companion(s)?

## PROMPT 11

Can you remember a time when you got locked out of where you needed to be?

**PROMPT 12**

Can you remember a time when you totally forgot an important date or appointment?

## PROMPT 13

Can you remember a time when your first impression of someone turned out to be completely wrong?

## PROMPT 14

Can you remember a time when you learned something from a child?

# PROMPT 15

Can you remember a problem with a haircut? ... Make-up? ... An article of clothing?

## PROMPT 16

Can you remember a time when you got a gift or a compliment which you did not at all deserve?

## PROMPT 17

Can you remember a time when you almost won, but not quite?

## PROMPT 18

Can you remember a time when you were tricked or lied to?

## SECTION III

## Recovering Memories Through Places

Just imagine that you have an older family member, say Grandma, who is now in her nineties and quite mentally competent though not very talkative. One day you decide to try to see if you can pull any interesting family stories out of this woman who has lived so long and whose memory must certainly be a library of experiences.

You go for a visit to the retirement community where Grandma is living. Once there, you find Grandma sitting in her chair, as always, seemingly dreaming away the afternoon. Maybe there is hope for a story. After all, she isn't watching soap operas right now. It's worth a try!

"Hello, Grandma!" you begin. She is glad to see you.

"I've just been thinking, Grandma, about your being ninety-four years old. You must have a lot of memories. How about telling me about some of the things you remember from long ago."

The first response is a blank look, followed soon my her usual answers: "No, I just can't remember anything ... nothing ever happened to me ... anyway, it wouldn't be interesting even if I could remember it."

Many people have reported a scenario very similar to this as the result of trying to pry information from family members who are surely old enough to be libraries of stories. Besides this, when most of us try to retrieve our own memories, we discover that we are soon thinking or saying the same things that Grandma said: "I just can't remember anything ... nothing ever happened to me ... it wouldn't be interesting even if I could remember."

Is this the end of the search for stories? Not at all!

The human mind is like an unlimited giant computer disk on which are stored all of the events, pictures, and impressions of our lives and experiences. Our quest is not to create what is not there; rather it is to find ways of accessing what we know must surely be lurking just around the corners and along the paths of our memories.

Throughout our lives our memories stay turned on, like a giant spinning computer disk, ready to hold more information than we can ever possibly store. The problem is that we store the memories of our lives without any formats. That is, the events of our lives are tossed at random into the vast storehouse of memory and when we go fishing for them we cannot know where to begin to look.

# SECTION III

From working with computers we may learn something which helps us out of this dilemma. That helpful insight is this: Memory recovery is never a one-step operation.

We cannot go to a computer keyboard and, in one step, retrieve randomly stored bits of information. No, computer memory recall always involves at least two steps.

First we must pull up the file in which the sought-for information has been stored, and then we can read out of that file the information which has been placed in it.

What this means, in terms of human memory recall, is that if we can find the files we will have greatly improved our chances of being able to read what is stored in them.

Now we are ready to work at identifying files and at practicing procedures for pulling memories out of them. We will keep in mind this primary principle:

*The physical places where events occurred are the memory files in which our minds most easily store the memories of important events that occurred in those physical places.*

Let's try this primary principal out on our retirement center visit to ninety-four-year-old Grandma.

"Grandma," we try it again.

"I know that you were married in 1921 ... isn't that right?"

"That's right," she answers, "on the sixteenth day of April."

"Well, Grandma," we continue, "I never saw that little house where you and Grandpa first set up housekeeping when you got married. I remember seeing one picture of it, but the house was gone before I was ever born.

"Grandma, can you still remember that little house on Maple Street?"

Her reply is instantaneous and even a bit annoyed. "Of course I remember it! You don't forget a place where you lived the first fifteen years of your married life. We raised three children in that house and one of them was your mother."

(This is more than she has talked in the last three visits! Maybe there is hope after all.)

We continue, "Well, Grandma, could you tell me about that little house, I mean, could you just sort of take me on a visit there and tell me what it looked like to live there?"

## SECTION III

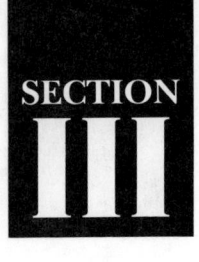

Grandma talks all afternoon.

First she takes us through the back door into the kitchen. Once she is, in her mind, back in that kitchen, the stories start to roll out. This is because when she took herself back to the place, she began to remember all of the important things which happened in that place. She even said that she could see them in her mind.

We heard about what happened at the stove, what happened over by the sink, what she saw out the window in that big snow of 1928, what happened at the table, the time that Grandpa nearly burned the house down. We had opened the "place file" and she was simply reading her memories out of it.

In the following set of exercises, we will use place prompts in the same way that we used plot prompts in the first series of exercises. Make use of them as you did then, hopefully in the context of a multi-generational family grouping, but on your own if that is not possible.

And have a good time traveling through the "places of memory."

## PROMPT 1

Take us with you when you had to move from one home to another.

**MORE IDEAS**

This prompt is still close to the plot prompts that we have been working with, in that moving is usually a crisis event and to take us to these two places puts us back inside the plot of a story. However, we are now more deliberately asking for place description. Note in this prompt the difference between the way the two places are described and the storyteller's feelings and relationship to the old and new homes.

## PROMPT 2

**Take us with you to a movie when you were a child or a teenager.**

**MORE IDEAS**

Can you remember specific movies? Were drive-in theatres or horror movies part of your past? How about movie snacks, spilled drinks, etc.?

## PROMPT 3

Take us on a walk around the neighborhood or rural area where you lived as a child.

**MORE IDEAS**

Be careful, when taking us through a widespread area, that you stand still in one place until we can see where we are to start with before we start moving. Give us a clear and visual beginning point, then sense that we are walking beside you, and you will be able to take us through a large space without our getting lost or confused.

## PROMPT 4

# Take us on a visit to your favorite childhood store.

**MORE IDEAS**

Don't forget that while we are starting with *places*, there are usually *people* in those places. Can you remember people who worked in your favorite store? Were you afraid of anyone who was there? And, who liked to go there with you?

## PROMPT 5

Take us on a childhood shopping trip with your mother or another family member.

**MORE IDEAS**

Observe that in this prompt we are coming close to looking at *place, person, and happening* all at the same time. As you tell your story, notice which of these three emerges as most central in the account of your memory.

## PROMPT 6

Take us on a visit to your childhood doctor's office.

**MORE IDEAS**

This may be a prompt in which the surroundings are more interesting memories than anything else. What kind of "primitive apparatus" or "mysterious equipment" do you remember? Try the same prompt as applied to the dentist or orthodontist. Older family members may tell about the family doctor's house call.

# PROMPT 7

Take us to school with you during one of your favorite years in school.

# MORE IDEAS

Related stories may include memories of your high school proms, your graduation from various school grade levels, your first day of school, or memories of final exams.

## PROMPT 8

Did you go to summer camp? Take us there for an afternoon, or even overnight.

**MORE IDEAS**

This prompt often reminds people of short-term and long-term friendships and sometimes of first kisses, summer loves, and early adventures with the opposite sex.

## PROMPT 9

**Can you take us to visit the place where your father or your mother worked?**

**MORE IDEAS**

All memorable workplaces may be usable place prompts. These include the places we ourselves have worked, especially those teenage summer jobs and those ways of earning money we would not want to have to do again.

# PROMPT 10

## Can you take us back home with you for a childhood holiday meal?

**MORE IDEAS**

Where did your family go for holiday meals? Did you go to a grandparent's house, or was your house the center of the family gathering? Was there a favorite place where your family liked to go out to eat for special occasions?

## SECTION III

## Let's Check On Where We Are

If you are experiencing even a moderate degree of success in discovering and telling your own new and original stories, predictable questions will eventually arise. "How should I preserve these wonderful stories that I am now finding and telling? Should I write them down, should I tape-record them? What should I do to save my creative work?"

If you are at the point of beginning to ask these questions, it is time to give some consideration to a more thorough understanding of the *language medium* in which the storyteller works and the implications the particular nature of that medium has for our interest in story preservation.

Because written language is made of words preserved for us on the printed page, we are often tempted to think that oral language is also made of words spoken out loud rather than written, and that the only difference between the written story and the oral story is the fact that one comes in through our eyes and the other through our ears. If this were true, it would be a simple thing to merely record the oral story and then transcribe what was told, and we would have the story in writing.

The nature of the storytelling medium is, however, not a medium made of words, and so the simple transcription process does not work well at all as a way to preserve storytelling.

In reality, when we *tell* a story to a living group of listeners, we are making use of *five* language dimensions whereas when we *write* we have only *one* to work with. Let's look at these five oral/kinesthetic language dimensions so that we may understand the storyteller's medium better, and so that we can grasp more clearly the documentation task and some of the issues related to moving from telling to writing.

### The Five Languages Of Storytelling

(1) Before and apart from words, the storyteller has a fully developed language of **gesture** to use in telling the story. Children acquire gestural language soon after birth, and throughout all our lives our gestural language remains not only usable but probably carries more of the content of our storytelling than do the words. For example, with gestural language alone we can show our listeners a list of all the musical instruments we wish we could play; without gesture it is almost impossible to tell another person what an accordion is. Gesture is one of our natural languages

## SECTION III

which we use in oral communication without ever even thinking about it.

(2) Apart from and in addition to words, there is a fully developed and usable language of **sound** which we make use of in telling our stories. Again, children acquire their ability to use sound (not words) soon after birth and exercise this sound-language through a range which runs from loud screaming to quiet giggling. A very young child can give the entire world a passing grade or a failing grade simply through the language of sound.

With sound-shaping we can give words which look the same on the printed page (no matter what they mean) a whole range of different meanings. Think of the word "mother." Any average teenager can shape the sound with which the word is spoken and give this simple word a dozen different meanings. Try the same with words like "fire," or even with a simple expletive like "oh."

Throughout all of our lives the language of sound remains a basic and usable natural language which we employ to supplement, bend, refine, and focus the meanings of the words that we use.

(3) A third natural language which we use in oral communication is the language of **attitude**. Our ability to subtly display attitude and emotion is a very powerful part of our functional kinesthetic language.

It is this dimension of our language through which the speaker reveals such things as whether he or she is happy with the audience at hand, whether the audience is liked or disliked, whether the speaker is confident about what is being said. It is almost impossible to cover up our natural display of feelings which range from boredom to excitement, and this "language" of displayed attitude and emotion in itself shapes and augments the content of the words which are spoken.

Most of our judgments about whether people around us are happy or sad, about whether they like us or not, are based on the language of attitude.

(4) There is still another language dimension which the storyteller makes use of apart from and in addition to words. This is the language phenomenon of being guided and molded by listener **feedback**.

When we tell our story to a group of present

# SECTION III

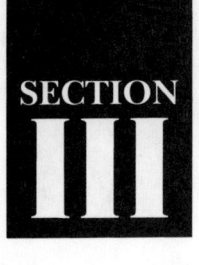

listeners, those listeners actually guide our telling by their responses. If our listeners look puzzled, we explain more fully what we are describing. If we receive a laugh of recognition, our story moves forward. If people begin to look bored, we quickly attempt to recapture their interest. Even though the teller has the floor, a great deal of the shape and content of the story is determined by the listeners.

Think of what we do when we want someone to come to our home for dinner and we begin to give them directions for finding where we live. We are the one who possesses all of the information they need to find our house, yet we begin with the question, "Where are you going to be coming from?" Even after that beginning question, we continue to check out every turn along the way to be sure that we have not "lost" them. The listener has guided and molded the teller.

It could even be said that it is the response of the parent which determines how long the baby cries. The listener has great power to influence the teller.

(5) At last we come to the **words**! (In addition to the above language dimensions, the storyteller

also gets to use words.) Now the tricky part begins!

*If* we are telling our story in person with a present group of listeners, we get to make use of all five of these storytelling language dimensions as we do so. As tellers we get to use gesture, sound, attitude, feedback response, and words as we move the story from our heads into the heads of our listeners.

*But*... suppose for a moment that we decide to record the stories being told for those members of the family not present to hear them told. What elements of the stories have those later listeners lost when they listen to the recording? They have, of course, lost all of the gestural language.

If we are aware of this, then we must compensate *in words* for what we could otherwise communicate to a present audience through gesture. (However, since the listener hears us tell the story to a live audience and hears the sounds they make in response to our telling, we still retain the use of attitude and feedback in this telling.)

Now... suppose that when we are all alone we try to tell our story *straight into a microphone* as an easy way to save it. Not only would anyone who lis-

## SECTION III

tens to it later be unable to see our gestures, we would also be without the feedback of any present listeners to help keep the story clear and guided. In addition, almost all of our ability to communicate through attitude and emotion is lost when we are all alone with the microphone.

The story told in this way must compensate *with more words* for all that is lost.

Finally, suppose that I decide to document my story *in writing*. In addition to the above losses, I also lose the ability to shape words with sound to give them particular refinements of meaning and emphasis. All that I now have to work with is the written word and I must work very hard to compensate fully for losing gesture, sound, attitude, and feedback, using additional words to more fully describe time and place, using additional words to identify who is speaking in the story and to whom, using words to declare attitudes and emotions, using words to make up for the entire loss of my body and my listeners as storytelling instruments.

So now... how shall we document our stories?

With recording? Maybe so, but if so, be very aware of the limitations the tape recorder has.

In writing? Maybe so, but if so, be very aware of the compensations which must be made, and the fact that the spoken word written down is now understood as neither telling nor writing.

Here are a few more place prompts to work with.

## PROMPT 11

**Can you take us to the one spot in all the world where you would like to have built a house?**

**PROMPT 12**

# Can you take us to visit your childhood hiding place or special thinking place?

# PROMPT 13

## Can you take us to a special place where you liked to go for walks or for picnics?

## PROMPT 14

Can you take us with you to visit a place you went only once but have always wanted to go back to again?

# SECTION III

## Additional Hints

Don't overlook these additional forms of story documentation:

(1) Draw a floor plan of the houses which are important in family stories, and make notes on the plan of important events or happenings. (You can do the same with schools and/or work places.)

(2) Find pictures of the kinds of cars, furniture, or appliances which form the time settings of your stories and make a scrapbook of them, even if you have no family photographs from that time period.

(3) Draw a map of the community or neighborhood in which your important family stories happen and make notes on the map about the location of important happenings.

(4) Make "flow charts" of the sequences of action in stories which you don't want to forget, but which are not quite clear enough to save in a completed form.

# SECTION IV

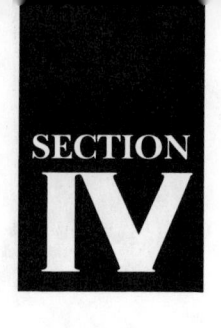

## Starting Stories With Memorable People

In the opening section we said that all family stories are about either *important happenings, important places, or important people.*

Now it is time to work with people.

This section has been held out until last for two specific reasons. The first is that most of us would think that stories about people are so much more important than stories about happenings or about places that we would jump to start right in with the people and never get beyond there. The choice to begin by working with happenings and places was made just for that reason. If we have to struggle in the beginning with the more difficult starting places (while we are still fresh) we will find stories we might otherwise have missed.

The real reason, though, is more subtle and more significant.

Most of the people in our strongest memories were so close to us that it is easy to assume that what we remember of them must surely be remembered by other members of our family. It is often much more difficult to describe the familiar because we cannot figure out what our hearers *do not know* and we hesitate to describe what we believe to be the obvious.

Now that we have had some practice with

telling and with working with prompts, we turn to person prompts, with some experience at both remembering and telling.

Notice how our telling now begins to "fall into stories" simply because we have learned a lot about what a story is and much about how to tell it to our listeners.

Work through the person prompts just as you did with the plot prompts and the place prompts. Remember again that "extended family" may include those who are not officially kin and at times may even include such non-human "relatives" as teachers, automobiles, and pets.

Can you help us to meet an important person whom we would never have a chance to know as you knew them? These prompts are a chance to do just that!

## PROMPT 1

Can you introduce us to the oldest person you can remember knowing when you were a child?

**MORE IDEAS**

Try using this prompt twice: once as you think about older people who were related to you, then again as you try to think about neighbors or friends who were not actually relatives.

## PROMPT 2

Can you tell us about an early friend whom you have continued to know all of your life?

**MORE IDEAS**

The most difficult stories to see are often those closest to us. It may not have occurred to us that our most important personal stories may be about those people who have always been there.

## PROMPT 3

**Can you tell us about an early friend whom you wonder what finally happened to?**

## MORE IDEAS

Sometimes the discovery of a story is the beginning of action! Have you or your family remembered, through the last two prompts, someone whom you might want to try to find or reestablish contact with? If you do, don't forget the story of the reunion which comes about.

# PROMPT 4

**Can you help us meet someone who used to come and visit at your house when you were growing up?**

**MORE IDEAS**

Remember what we learned earlier about descriptive skills. How did this person travel to come to see you? What did they normally wear? And ... when and where did this visit actually take place?

# PROMPT 5

## Can you introduce us to a teacher to whom you owe a lot?

**MORE IDEAS**

Teacher stories seem to abound! Don't forget your favorite "teacher from hell," on the negative side, as well as those teachers you had whom you wish your own children or grandchildren might have. While you're at it, don't forget the principals, school janitors, and school secretaries.

## PROMPT 6

**Can you introduce us to a girlfriend or boyfriend whom you did not marry?**

# MORE IDEAS

One of the delightful things about family stories comes when we begin to enjoy the diverse ways in which different generations deal with similar situations and issues. Learning to laugh at our innocent differences in values may emerge as an interesting part of our storytelling experience.

**PROMPT 7**

# Can you remember the first person you ever had a crush on?

**MORE IDEAS**

This prompt may be pursued chronologically throughout one's growing-up years and may produce a series of personalities and a matching number of stories.

# SECTION IV

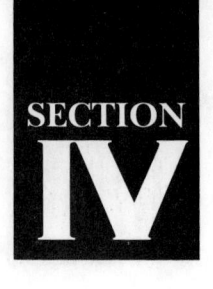

## Let's Check On Where We Are

At this time we may be noticing once again that we are coming up with what seem to be many story fragments without being able to feel that any whole stories are emerging. If this is true for you or your family, go back and review "A Story Form Format" (page 36) and remind yourself of the plot elements necessary for a full story that works. Now, as we continue to meet new people, look carefully at whether we are having them go through all of the steps required for a successfully plotted story. This may give us an additional set of questions to ask about each of the people we are now working to tell about.

### Storytelling as Identity Maintenance

*(Or ... why do we find stories where we find them?)*

| Fortune Seeking | Identity Maintenance |
|---|---|

▲

The basic function of storytelling is **identity maintenance**. In other words, we tell stories to remind ourselves of who we are and to tell other people who we are.

For example, we may be the family that tells the story about how grandfather and grandmother survived the flood of 1887. At each holiday gathering the story must be told again and again. Other stories begin to be added on for later generations.

When new friends are added to our family circle, at some point they must hear the story of the flood of 1887. Once we know that they have heard our family stories, we feel that we have told them who we are.

But, we are not single-story families. The total identity of our family is contained in many stories, some of which are different for some family members and some of which take on varying degrees of importance at various times. As a whole, however, we tell stories to define and expand the concept of who we are.

This identity function is seen as being strongly operative in emerging national and cultural groups. The narratives of the Old Testament are the stories told by the people of Israel both to

# SECTION IV

remind themselves and to tell others who they are. We find the same to be true as we look at other traditional/cultural literature, both oral and written, at various time periods around the world.

Wherever we find a person or a group of people who have a strong primary concern with identity, we will find stories and storytelling. This is true today as well as in past generations.

In the graphic at the beginning of this section you will see a figure that looks like a seesaw. On one end of the seesaw are the words *identity maintenance*, that functional definition of storytelling which we have just sketchily summarized.

A quick look at the other end of the seesaw will show us how to spot places, both in terms of individual interest and community priorities, where storytelling does not exist. Put simply, when a person or a community is more interested in *fortune seeking* than in identity maintenance, stories are left behind and storytelling dies.

This simple distinction between fortune seeking and identity maintenance may be seen in many instances as we look at it on both macrocosmic and microcosmic levels.

On the macrocosmic level, we will notice that

we find storytelling alive in small towns and communities where "who we are" is more important than "what we do." We do not find storytelling alive in growing urban communities where we have moved both to seek our fortune and to get away from where we grew up.

We find stories alive and well in age groups of people who have either made their fortune and are now asking "who are we?" or have given up on making their fortune and have discovered that identity is more important anyway. We do not find much real storytelling in those competitive age groups in which people are individualistically trying to get ahead of one another.

Storytelling is alive within groups of migrating peoples who are moving in order to maintain and preserve who they are. We do not find storytelling with individual immigrants who have left home to get away from an old life. They may even change their names, change their language, and change as much of their physical appearance (hair styles, makeup, dress) as possible. They are blending into a new world to make their fortune, and the stories of where they came from do not contribute to this.

The microcosmic version of this phenomenon

# SECTION IV

is the series of developmental stages each of us goes through in the course of our lives. As children, the stories shared within our family are comforting to us and help us to form our basic identity and to know who we are as a family group. But when we enter adolescence and then young adulthood, we tend to abandon the family stories, including their values and structures and habits, as we step out into our own lives and seek the personal identity associated with seeking our own fortune. At this time in our development, we are apt to tell others very little about where we came from.

In midlife we tend to rediscover the importance of affirming and maintaining our own identity, and we begin to ask questions which are answered through the recovery and telling of our family stories.

The seesaw graphic is apt. On a seesaw, when weight is shifted toward one end it moves away from the other end. Similarly, the more strongly we move toward either fortune seeking or identity maintenance, the more strongly we leave the opposite behind. We may, however, compartmentalize our lives, so that we, for example, seek our fortunes by day and maintain our identities by night! We sometimes see this phenomenon in ethnic communities or neighborhoods where people go out to seek their fortune, then return home to care for who they are.

Think of this overall concept in respect to your own family experience with storytelling, and see whether it is helpful to you in understanding different people's attitudes toward and participation in the family story.

Here are a few more person prompts to bring memories to life.

# PROMPT 8

Can you tell us about a memorable person you once worked with? Or a memorable person you once worked for?

## PROMPT 9

Can you tell us about a person who once had something that you wanted?

# PROMPT 10

Can you tell us about a person whom you wanted to be like when you grew up?

## PROMPT 11

Can you tell us about a person at whose home you sometimes spent the night?

## PROMPT 12

### Can you tell us about the person for whom you were named?

## PROMPT 13

If you haven't done so yet, can you tell us about one of your grandmothers or grandfathers?

# PROMPT 14

# Can you introduce us to someone at your class reunion?

## SECTION V

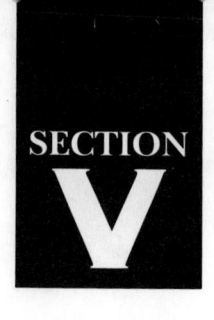

## Who Can We Ask About?

As stated at the beginning of Section II, many of us have older family members who are still living from whom we could probably get a lot of information if we knew what to ask. That entire section was built on asking questions about places.

Now that we have just been dealing with people in the last section, let us look at an additional process that may help us discover further questions about people which may be directed to older family members. This process deals with figuring out **who we can ask questions about** as we talk with those who are still with us.

On the following two pages we find a format for a Family Lifespan Chart. This chart may be duplicated, if several people want to work with it separately. Look at the chart format, then follow the directions for personalizing it for your family cast of characters. Questions and suggestions for use will then follow.

INSTRUCTIONS: On the chart you will plot the lifespans of each member of your own family cast of characters. Begin with yourself, then move, in terms of closeness of kin, to as many members of your family as you can think of. You may need to consult family records to do this accurately. Do not stop with only those people whom you personally remember. List grandparents, great-aunts, cousins, and so on, whom you never knew. Your cast of characters includes those who were born before you (whose lifespans will begin to the left) as well as those who were born later (whose lifespans will be more to the right). Adding the date(s) of birth and/or death after each family member's name may be helpful.

# SECTION V

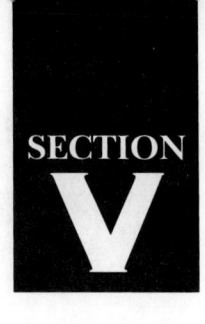

# Create A Timeline

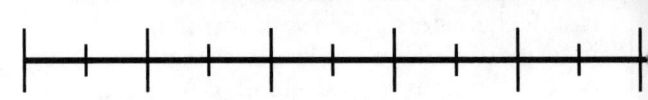

|—+—+—+—+—+—+—+—+—|

At this end, put the date abtained by subtracting
your present age from your year of birth.

## Family Lifespan Chart

**YOUR FATHER**

**YOUR MOTHER**

Continue this process with all siblings, aunts and uncles, cousins, and even significant friends or neighbors if they seem to fit in. Be sure to include persons whose lives were limited including children who died very young. If making one chart for a whole family, use the birth date of the oldest person present as the center line for the chart.

# For Your Family

├──┼──┼──┼──┼──┼──┼──┼──┤

In the middle, put your own date of birth.

At this end, put this year's date.

**YOURSELF**

**YOUR SISTER**

The following pages includes ideas for using this information.

# SECTION V

## Using The Lifespan Chart

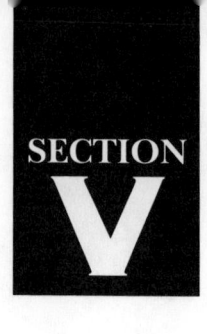

As you look at the lifespan chart which you have created, begin to notice several things:

■ Notice short lines and long lines. We have illustrated right before our eyes short lives and long lives. It is probable that some of the short lines may represent people who tend to be forgotten when our family stories are told. What happened to the people whose lives are represented by short lines?

■ Begin to notice that many of the people in our family cast of characters are no longer living. We may often forget them unless we notice that a great deal of their lifelines overlap our own lifelines. Are there stories to be remembered when we look at causes of death relative to those people who have finished their lives prior to now?

■ Notice naming patterns. What are the favorite names which seem to occur over and over again in your family? Is there a pattern by which names carry on from generation to generation? Do the names which appear show you anything about your family's cultural place of origin or ancestry? Are there names which disappear for one reason or another? Where did each name actually come from?

■ Take the lifelines of those older family members who are still living and look carefully at the other lives that they overlap which the younger relatives know nothing about. This may be the most valuable thing about doing this chart. We may discover that there are people we never knew to ask about whom our present older relatives remember quite well–if we only knew to ask about them.

■ Look at each person's name and lifeline. Are there particular questions you have about that person? Is there anyone still alive who might be able to offer a clue to answering that question?

■ Look back at the chart now, and see whether you want to add more names and lines to it now that you have thought about it for this bit of time.

# SECTION VI

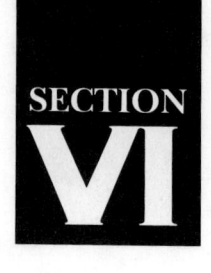

## An Afterword About Fiction And Family Storytelling

As students in elementary school we are taught that the difference between nonfiction and fiction is that nonfiction is "true" and fiction is "made-up." The aspiring writer must overcome the inadequacy of this elementary definition in order to take advantage of his or her personal experiences and knowledge in creating fiction.

The reality is that, if we pay careful attention, the more we learn about the lives and experiences of our favorite fiction writers the more we see how strongly fiction imitates and expands upon and is, indeed, inspired by real life. In fact, the more fiction is based upon reality the more believable it is. It is quickly obvious that the medical novel written by the physician and the courtroom drama written by the attorney are more believable and alive than such attempts by the professional writer.

What this means is that honestly stepping over into fiction may be the answer to dealing with and handling some of those stories which are either too incomplete in memory or too sensitive in nature to be told straightforwardly as family history.

When we have large gaps in memory or when we want to protect the innocent, this does not necessarily mean that the richness of such material must be either deliberately buried or forever lost. Rather, consider making use of such strong fragments as beginning places or seeds for what we truthfully label as fiction.

The test is one of honesty. If the family story can be told to or in the presence of those who knew the main characters, for example, and if they nod their heads as they listen and say things like, "That's the kind of person Grandma was," then we are clearly dealing with good family storytelling.

But ... if there is uncertainty and disagreement and a feeling that we might tell a certain story only when a long way from home, then it may be time to honestly move into fiction. With new names and new settings, many good stories may be more appropriately handled as "a story based on" a certain person or experience rather than claiming any pretense to biographical reality.

Truth is a good thing to wrestle with in family storytelling. It is a different issue altogether to wrestle with perspective and point of view. Wrestle carefully, and hard, and honestly ... and then the story told has its own integrity, whether it be candidly labeled fiction or nonfiction.

*Donald Davis Books and Audiobooks from August House*

**See Rock City**
*A Story Journey through Appalachia*
Hardback / ISBN 0-87483-448-1
Paperback / ISBN 0-87483-456-2
Audiobook / ISBN 0-87483-452-X

**Listening for the Crack of Dawn**
*A Master Storyteller Recalls the Appalachia of the 50's & 60's*
Paperback / ISBN 0-87483-130-X
Audiobook / ISBN 0-87483-147-4

**Barking at a Fox-Fur Coat**
*Family stories to keep you laughing into the next generation*
Hardback / ISBN 0-87483-140-7
Paperback / ISBN 0-87483-087-7

**Stanley Easter**
*A young man's love-hate relationship with his hometown
proves you can go home again*
Audiobook / ISBN 0-87483-505-4

**Dr. York, Miss Willie and the Typhoid Shot**
Audiobook / ISBN 0-87483-506-2

*August House Publishers P.O. Box 3223 Little Rock, AR 72203
800-284-8784 / order@augusthouse.com*

*Dee Brown's "My Arkansas Memories" continued*

The arm was broken. I was rushed to one of the doctors there in Stephens. He probably did me a great favor by admitting that the multiple fracture was out of his league. I would need to be sent to Camden, where the arm could be X-rayed before it could be set properly. I was placed on the train, sent to Camden, and the arm was set. But the ram's days were then numbered.

Still, he was a pet, almost like a member of the family, and we could not quite bring ourselves to roast him or sell him — if a buyer could be found. It was old Mrs. Valentine who sealed the ram's fate. She did it by going to church. Actually, she did it by stopping off at our house to pick up my aunt on her way to church. I don't recall what Mrs. Valentine was wearing on that trip to prayer meeting, but it attracted the ram's attention. He applied his hard head to the usual spot on that old woman's anatomy, sending her sprawling into a flowering bush beside our porch steps. Mrs. Valentine, being a Christian lady, forgave the Browns but not their pet. Now the ram's days were seriously numbered. Hog-killing time came with cold weather, and the ram was counted among the swine. I couldn't watch, because he had been a pet and because I secretly felt responsible, due to my taunting.

## ■ Junie's House ■

A small four-room house stood roughly between our yard and our barnyard. It had been built in earlier days by an uncle, now deceased, to house an aging servant couple, also long gone. My mother let a black family live there for free.

I remember the small house because it housed one of my favorite childhood playmates. Junie and I were about the same age and — sharing both a yard and a barnyard — we found common entertainment easily. We did until some age of reason — or unfortunate socialization — led us each to realize that we were not of the same race. I don't remember how old we were or if there was any catalyst for our realization. Mostly I recall the sense of unspoken loss that followed, too early to be described as adolescent angst and too much a taboo to allow for any dialogue or discussion with adults.

Junie's parents were enterprising, each in their own way. June, the father, wore a white jacket to his job running the dining room of the Stephens Hotel. The hotel served mostly as a rooming house for drummers, traveling salesmen who arrived and departed by train from Little Rock or Texarkana. On Sundays, however, families in their church finery would have dinner there. June was a handsome man, erect and alert, and the figure he cut in his starched white jacket lent the dining experience an aura we would only years later come to name sophistication.

The kitchen of the little house was Junie's mother's pride and joy. A canning factory had recently gone out of business and left behind hundreds of bright labels, the kind made to wrap around a metal can. They were tomato labels, with a huge, bright red tomato that seemed to float over an equally bright white background. Junie's mom had procured enough of those labels to paper her entire kitchen. My mother and her confidantes didn't seem to agree, but I thought it was the most dazzling room I'd ever seen.

# ■ Kaiser Wilhelm Came to Stephens ■

I must have been nine years old when the Armistice was declared ending the first World War. That evening we heard there was to be a gathering in the schoolyard. I ran the five blocks with my cousins. Everyone was there; it seemed the whole town had turned out for what I discovered was a burning in effigy of Kaiser Wilhelm. The ringleader was the Baptist minister.

Probably fifty of the eighty families in town had sons in the Army, Army Air Corps, Navy, or Marines. I had uncles at army bases around the country, and on transport ships right then, on their way to Europe. We were all worried about them, until suddenly — in one day — we knew the killing had stopped. I knew my mother was worried about my sister's husband, who was an airplane mechanic serving in France.

That night it seemed all the town was expressing pure relief, as all eyes turned to the dummy of the Kaiser staked up in the middle of a bonfire. The head was made of papier mâché — it must have been an all-day project — and he was uniformed, with a sash and everything, just as we saw the Kaiser in newspapers.

Shouts and cheers surrounded us. A few onlookers were silent, though. One was a young man who had just returned from France where he had been gassed in trench warfare. He didn't live long after the war, because no one knew how to treat poison gas in those days. In spite of everything, that was a night of celebration. I remember seeing the bonfire reflected in the big panes of the schoolhouse windows.

## ■ Hattie Caraway ■

During the Depression, for those of us who had just graduated from college in Arkansas, there were no jobs to be found locally. As a new graduate of Arkansas State Teachers College (now UCA), I did what hundreds of Arkansas college grads did at the time; I went to Washington, D.C. There wasn't a lot of work there, either, but there was more. Since government workers ate lunch out more than office workers in other cities, there were restaurant jobs to be had, even if for just a few hours a day, peeling potatoes before lunch or washing thick pottery plates and mugs after. At twenty-five cents an hour, it was enough to keep you from starving, if you were lucky enough to have found a fellow Arkie who would let you sleep on the floor of his small apartment.

Another source of occasional employment in Washington was Senator Hattie Caraway. Forget Joe T. Robinson; he scorned job-seekers innocent enough to knock on his office door. But Hattie Caraway and her two staff assistants seemed to see us as a challenge. Every morning, Mrs. Caraway would pick up the phone and call the trucking companies who had contracts to bring paper, office supplies, and other consumables into the district from outlying warehouses. She would identify herself and ask if there was not a shipment that needed to be unloaded that morning. If a dispatcher told her that the driver was expected to unload his truck, Senator Caraway told him that printing paper was heavy, that surely the driver needed another man to help. Due to her cajoling, several of us Arkansas college grads found day labor on a regular basis.

The work was hard, and at twenty-five cents an hour, the best we hoped for was to go home with two dollars in our pocket, but in those days two dollars would buy a pair of pants or enough food for a week.

## ■ Nearly a Restaurant Magnate ■

During the early days of the Great Depression, I worked at lunch counters on occasion. During this time, I heard that the operator of several A&W franchises in the District of Columbia was opening a new hot shop to introduce barbecue to Washington. Immediately I walked to the location, just opened by a young man who introduced himself as J.W. Marriott. I almost regretted being hired when the other employees told me how he watched the restaurant like a hawk. But a regular job was rare and I was determined to stick it out.

My job started in the evening when girls took orders from cars and delivered food on trays that hinged on the driver's window. Marriott told me that he was sometimes cheated by drivers who would become impatient while his waitress worked another car and would drive off without paying. So he named me "curb master" and had me watch to be sure that collections were made — often by me — when a car was ready to leave but its waitress was otherwise engaged.

I found that Marriott did, indeed, watch the shop like a hawk. I saw him fire people for drinking milkshakes on duty. One night he showed up unexpectedly at midnight. When the manager was found to be off-site, Marriott was obviously displeased. The manager was never seen again, and word had it that he was sent packing back to his home in Utah.

Several of the young men who worked in the shop found the regular pay compensated for Marriott's intensity, though we often caught ourselves thinking, *Is this what I spent four years in college preparing for?* One young man especially resented working below his training. He had a degree from Massachusetts Institute of Technology and felt that even a Depression economy should not stand between him and appropriate employment. He later got a job driving a taxi, which could not have paid much more, but he at least felt vindicated by the new job.

We men made our best money after midnight because Mr. Marriott sent all the girls home then. Then we waited on cars and collected the tips. Some of those late-night customers were pretty good tippers, by Depression standards.

I left Marriott's shop to take a job in the Food and Drug Administration. Marriott told me that I was foolish for leaving his organization to take a government job. He scolded me, saying he was going to open dozens of hot shops just like that one; it would make me a wealthy man if I stayed with him. I knew that I would never have a moment's peace if I worked for him, and the government job looked too good to pass up. But he was right about his business: people came from miles around to eat his barbecue sandwiches.

## ■ The New Deal Days ■

While I was living in Washington, D.C., I watched as idealistic men and women who wanted to put Roosevelt's Four Freedoms into public policy set up the many agencies of the New Deal. We were all idealistic, even in our after-work activities. Groups would gather in the evenings to discuss any number of social problems and to argue — often for hours — about the best solutions.

There were literary meetings, too. I often attended those, sometimes held in an apartment, sometimes a meeting room at a church or YMCA. Occasionally a well-known writer would show up, not as part of a planned program but just out of personal interest. That was how I met Sherwood Anderson, who was then famous for his novel *Winesburg, Ohio*. I must have gushed something about not expecting to meet someone famous in my neighborhood, because he said, "You can't be famous in Washington, D.C. Everyone here is famous, therefore no one is."

We struck up a friendship after that chance meeting. At least we were well enough acquainted that I stopped to visit him in southwest Virginia for a day on my first visit back to Arkansas. The Southern Railway ran from Washington to New Orleans, and the little town in which Anderson had bought two newspapers was one of the stops. I was probably the only one to get off there. I found him at the little newspaper office that now housed what had once been two competing newspapers.

Anderson took me to lunch and explained that he had always wanted to own a country newspaper (also a juvenile dream of my own — to own and run an Arkansas country weekly). His advice was that I should give up the dream, because, as he explained from his own experience, he would never have been able to afford the newspapers but for the luck of his novel becoming a bestseller.

Anderson had an innovative business plan for his two newspapers: they were identical in content, except for the editorial page. One paper paid a prominent Republican to write its weekly editorial and the other paper did the same with a prominent Democrat. That way, Anderson himself did the courthouse beat. Why? Because he enjoyed it. He might report on a murder trial, a swindler's demise, or a divorce. You could always tell his reportage by his vocabulary and pacing. A Sherwood Anderson divorce notice might share a few juicy tidbits and wry asides; it was a thing of beauty.

After my lunch with Mr. Anderson I was back on the platform awaiting the next southwest-bound passenger train, heading home to Arkansas, a little wiser for the visit.

## ■ The Second Time Is a Charm ■

I made two trips home via the Southern Railway during the New Deal days. Both times I was looking for work back in my home state. Washington was exciting for a young man, but I was homesick. During both visits, I was met at the train station in Little Rock by one of the two or three uncles who owned an automobile, still a rare luxury in Stephens, Arkansas.

After a visit with relatives around a dinner table heaped with steaming bowls of vegetables and platters of fried chicken, I ventured to Little Rock in hopes of finding work. There was surely nothing befitting a graduate of Arkansas State Teachers College to be had in Stephens.

There wasn't in Little Rock, either. It was the Depression, after all.

I started my first trip with high hopes by visiting all of Little Rock's printing companies, since I was a trained typesetter and press operator. There was nothing. I looked for work in the usual manual pursuits, such as loading and unloading trucks. There was nothing. Reluctantly, I boarded the train back to my colorless job in Washington.

When time came for my second visit home, I had a plan. I had by then spent some time working in the Department of Agriculture in Washington, and I knew that the "3 C's" — the Civilian Conservation Corps — was working quite a few sites in Arkansas. After the ritual visit in Stephens, I set my sights on the CCC office in the YMCA building on Broadway in Little Rock. Though the building, with its Moorish arches and big swimming pool, was in its heyday, the CCC office was as drab as any government outpost you might imagine. Luck was with me though, and I was — probably in no small part because of my Washington experience — signed up at thirty dollars per month and sent to the camp outside Hot Springs. Thirty dollars a month was big money during the Depression, and I could be reasonably sure my government check would not bounce.

In camp, I was issued the standard CCC uniform, surplus World War I fatigues in one hundred percent wool. It was January at the time, and the wool shirt and trousers, though scratchy, were comfortable enough. Then along came a typical Arkansas March, and the wool became a portable sauna — with "splinters" of coarse wool. With every swing of an axe or pull of a saw, those surplus clothes felt worse than a blanket of sandpaper.

Then came the revelation that transformed my CCC experience and helped me forget about the apparel. A directive came from the central office in Little Rock requiring me to report to duty as a clerk without delay. When filling out my application, I had checked the box indicating that I could type, and a typist was needed to keep up with the many reports generated there.

My one distinguishing service to the CCC as a clerk-typist was the addition of a word to the bureaucratic lexicon. Turnover was high among the recruits in Arkansas, especially among those young men who hailed from the Great Plains. Why so many were sent from the Dakotas, Iowa, and Nebraska to the oak-canopied ravines and river bottoms overlaid with southern white pine and giant cypress remains a mystery to this day. To many of those northern recruits who were accustomed to sleeping with an uninterrupted view of the stars, the trees of Arkansas were not a handsome sight. They were a cause for concern, for worry, for anxiety. It was amazing how many of those Dakota boys became nervous wrecks sleeping under a pine tree.

I was awakened every morning before sunrise from my comfortable iron bunk in a warehouse along the railroad tracks in the east end of Little Rock by a retired Army sergeant who was determined to shape us Arkansas boys into a proper military unit. He called us his "Algerian Army"; we never knew why. The sergeant delivered us, after a proper reveille and a poor breakfast, to our clerical jobs on Broadway.

At my desk, which I was always aware was in the same building as a large swimming pool, I typed the release forms for the Dakota boys who'd had enough of trees. The kindly old colonel who, as near as I could tell, did nothing all day but sign forms and initial reports, thought me a champion of the cause when I replaced the traditional lengthy explanation for these particular releases with a single word: *arborphobia*. I don't know to this day if a linguist would acknowledge any such word, but for eighteen months during the New Deal, its five syllables shone like an infantryman's brass badge on my Army surplus fatigues and maintained my favor in the eyes of that old colonel.

Dee Brown of Little Rock is the author of over 25 books, including the seminal *Bury My Heart at Wounded Knee*. Born in 1908 in Stephens, Arkansas, he lived in Little Rock and Washington, D.C. before becoming an agricultural librarian at the University of Illinois.

## About the Author

Donald Davis has been seen on CNN, Nightline, and heard on National Public Radio. He is a perennial audience favorite at the National Storytelling Festival and other venues coast-to-coast. His many books include *Southern Jack Tales*, *Listening for the Crack of Dawn*, and *See Rock City*. His audio recordings of Southern storytelling include *Stanley Easter, Miss Daisy*, and *Christmas at Grandma's*. All of his books and recordings are available online at www.augusthouse.com. Mr. Davis and his wife, Merle, live on Ocracoke Island, off the North Carolina coast.